Birthd

Collect all the Magic Trix *books*

Birthday Wishes

Sara Grant

Illustrated by Erica-Jane Waters

Orion
Children's Books

First published in Great Britain in 2013
by Orion Children's Books
a division of the Orion Publishing Group Ltd
Orion House
5 Upper St Martin's Lane
London WC2H 9EA
An Hachette UK company

1 3 5 7 9 10 8 6 4 2

A catalogue record for this book is
available from the British Library.

ISBN 978 1 4440 0781 7

Printed in Great Britain by Clays Ltd, St Ives plc

To Miss Elliott, her class and everyone at
Kelvedon Hatch Primary School

Chapter One

"Slobber from a spotless Dalmatian?" Lulu asked her witches-in-training. She held up a glass jar filled with a cloudy thick liquid.

Trix's brain felt gooey, as if Lulu's lesson on magical mixtures had somehow turned her mind into a treacle sponge soaked in custard. Trix had recently turned ten years old and discovered she had the gift of magic. Every week day, she and four other new witches took lessons from Lulu on how to use their magical powers.

What potion would use dog slobber?

"It's a key ingredient for many stain-removing potions," Stella piped up. She smiled a horribly smug smile. She was right and she knew it. There was nothing wrong with right answers, but Stella made her rightness seem oh so wrong.

"That is correct!" Lulu exclaimed and returned the jar with its sloshing contents to the bookcase. Lulu picked up what appeared to be an empty jar. "Does anyone remember what this is?"

Trix hoped that wasn't the stink of a skunk. Lulu had opened the burp of a walrus at the beginning of the lesson and the fishy smell still lingered in the magic classroom.

"Eerie silence from outer space," Pippa

answered with a satisfied swish of her high ponytail.

Trix raised her eyebrows in surprise. When had Pippa become a genius at potions?

"Well done," Trix echoed Lulu's praise of her friend.

Over the past week, Lulu had taught them about the weird and wonderful ingredients stored in the magic classroom's huge bookcase. Lulu was responsible for training the newest witches in the Sisterhood of Magic in the hope that they would become fairy godmothers one day.

Today Lulu had surprised them with a quiz. The girls sat facing her, raising their hands when they knew the answer. Each witch had a magical familiar as a companion. All the familiars sat quietly on their witches' laps – except Trix's familiar. Jinx – her cheeky black and white kitten – scampered about the room as if dancing some strange cat jig to imaginary music.

Lulu asked question after question. After a little thought, Cara knew the recipe for the classic laughing potion. Then Lulu asked Becka's familiar, Sherlock the owl, to point his wing to each ingredient on the top shelf, and Becka guessed every single item correctly.

"Trix, which potion requires water off a duck's back and a tornado swirl?" Lulu held up a jar with a grey funnel cloud inside. The jar vibrated in her hands. "And it must be mixed with the tears of a tiger at the stroke of midnight."

Creeping cats! Potions were too much like science experiments. Mr Beaker had made Trix sit at the back of the class whenever he was performing an experiment. She had melted his glasses once and, ever since, he'd declared her a safety hazard when it came to science.

Trix begged her brain to be smarter.

"Come on, Trix," Stella moaned. "This is an easy one."

Oooooh, Stella made her so mad! She was embarrassing Trix in front of Lulu and the other witches. Trix didn't know the right answer but, even so, Stella's behaviour was unforgivable.

Wait! That's it!

"That's the recipe for a forgiveness potion!"
Trix exclaimed, smiling. Jinx leaped onto
Trix's lap. His spots sparkled like they always
did when he was proud of Trix.

"Magically marvellous!" Lulu spun in
a circle, setting the lacy hem of her gown
swishing at her ankles and the bracelets on
her wrists jingle-jangling. "Now let's review
a few of the spells that must accompany

certain potions," Lulu said when she stopped spinning. She lifted the biggest book off the bookcase and plonked it on a nearby table.

Lulu continued her lesson but her words seemed to float like clouds over Trix's head. It was hard to concentrate when Trix had a super-duper secret – tomorrow she was throwing her best friend Holly a surprise birthday party.

She usually hated keeping secrets. She told Holly everything – well, everything except the fact that she was a witch. Now, Holly was turning ten and Trix was sure – OK, she wasn't one hundred per cent certain, but she did hope, pray and wish with every cell in her body and every spark in her brain – that Holly would discover she was a witch too, just like Trix had on the night of her tenth birthday.

Trix's body felt like a shaken fizzy drink ready to explode. She shivered off her excitement and tried to concentrate on Lulu's lesson.

"What's that?" Pippa pointed to a bowl

half-full of white cubes made of teeny tiny crystals that reflected the green glow of Lulu's cauldron. Pippa's familiar, Twitch, a lavender rat, scuttled over and sniffed the white substance.

"Oh, that." Lulu popped one of the cubes in her mouth.

Trix's eyes narrowed and she gagged a little as she imagined the awful possibilities. Was that the dandruff from a meerkat? Ash from an erupting volcano? Freeze-dried dragon scales?

Lulu laughed when she spotted the pained expression on Trix's face. "They're sugar lumps for my tea." Lulu placed the sugar bowl on the shelf by her rainbow-striped teapot. "I can see your brains are overflowing with witch-tastic knowledge," Lulu said, straightening the rows and rows of jars. "And that's enough for this magically magnificent lesson. Have wonderful weekends, my dears!"

As Trix turned to go, something terrible happened in what felt like painfully slow motion. Her brain screamed that it couldn't be real, but her eyes showed that it definitely and dreadfully was . . .

Stella elbowed past Trix, which caused her to slip on a drop of rainbow essence Lulu had spilled earlier. As she went crashing to the floor, Trix knocked the bookcase. It wobbled and the glass jars clinked on the shelves. For a moment, the bookcase and its magical contents seemed to hover in the precarious place between tipping and falling.

Trix squeezed her eyes shut, covered her head and wondered if she was about to be squashed!

Chapter Two

"*WOLS OM!*" The words were screamed quickly and Lulu's voice cracked with the effort. She skidded to a stop next to Trix with her arms out wide as if she might catch the heavy bookcase.

But the strangest thing happened – or *didn't* happen.

The bookcase didn't fall.

Trix opened one eye and then the other.

Jars, bottles, boxes and bags were suspended in the air above her. Tasmanian devil sweat was frozen in a jar that dangled over her head.

Lulu seemed to have pushed pause on the world.

But that was impossible!

Lulu quickly righted the bookcase. The familiars rushed to her aid. Jinx jumped and shifted the jars back into place while Twitch and Rascal straightened the items on the lower shelf and Sherlock flapped between the top shelves. Trix and all the other new witches were too shocked to move or speak.

"Magic marbles!" Lulu exclaimed when the room seemed to come back to life a moment later. "I shouldn't have done that."

"Did the world stop or did we speed up?" Pippa asked.

"I used advanced magic." Lulu's face was as pale as her silvery curls. It was the first time Trix had seen Lulu shaken. "I had to save Trix."

Stella trailed her hand along the jars now resting safely on the shelf. "How does advanced magic work?"

"You utter the appropriate advanced magic spell. In this case, I said *wols om* and time stopped." Lulu shook her head. "No, that's not exactly right, time doesn't stop. It slows down for about a minute. It only works in confined spaces and affects the people and things immediately around the enchantress, and—"

"But *we* didn't slow down," Becka interrupted.

"Witches and familiars are immune – so they can move about freely during the spell," Lulu explained. "You won't learn advanced magic for quite some time. You only use this special spell in extreme emergencies. It's very tricky and there are lots of rules when you mess with the space-time continuum."

Space-time continuum? That sounded important and slightly scary.

"In other words, please don't use it," Lulu finished. She then explained how the next few minutes would actually speed up at an imperceptible rate until time had readjusted itself.

As Lulu bid farewell to her witches, Trix couldn't help but mentally repeat the spell: *wols om.* It was so simple! With it, she could stop a splat of spaghetti sauce from landing on her new white sweater. Or she could thwart her pesky younger brother, Oscar, the next time he tried to pull a mean trick on her – such as dipping her ponytail in blackcurrant jam or targeting her with a mud grenade.

Trix looked at Stella and realised she wasn't the only one dazzled by the possibilities. But while Trix was thinking of how to *stop* bad things from happening, Stella's evil grin suggested that she had realised all the ways the spell could *cause* trouble.

"Chloe and Lucy are definitely yeses!" Pippa said and put a tick by each of their names in her notebook.

Trix and Pippa were huddled together in Trix's lounge, going over last-minute preparations for tomorrow's party while Jinx chased Twitch and then Twitch chased Jinx. Trix and Pippa had raced home after school to finalise their top-secret plans for Holly's surprise party. They'd told Holly that they were staying after school to work on a special project for their Arts and Crafts class. Holly didn't know that Arts and Crafts was really a cover for Lulu's lessons in witchcraft.

"Grace, Sophie and Emma are coming, too," Pippa said, double-checking the invitation list for the birthday sleepover.

"Holly's mum is going to send Holly over here at six p.m. sharp," Trix explained. Trix had worked out all the details with Holly's parents. Early tomorrow, they were going to secretly bring over Holly's pyjamas and favourite pillow – and some treats for the sleepover, too. Then they were going to take Holly out for the day so that she wouldn't arrive early and ruin the big surprise.

Trix held her big green watch near Pippa's delicate pink one and checked the time on both. "Watches synchronised!" she declared and scribbled that item off the to-do list she had written on the back of a chocolate bar wrapper.

"Our watches are sink-row-*what*?" Pippa asked, her eyebrows crunching together in confusion. "Is that a big name for stylish?"

Trix tapped her watch. "It means our watches both say exactly the same time, so we can—"

The front door knob twisted and jingled the Christmas bells Trix had hung there earlier as a Holly warning system. Was that Holly? Trix crammed her list into the pocket of her school blazer, and Pippa closed her notebook with a snap.

"Hey, weirdo and weirder!" Oscar called as he closed the front door with a bang.

Trix relaxed. "Oh, it's only you."

"Who did you think it was," Oscar sing-songed, "Santa Claus?" Then Oscar's eyes widened and he rushed to the stairs. Trix hadn't noticed until now that a package was sitting on the bottom step. He scooped up the bright orange box and raced upstairs, shouting, "Leave me alone. I've got important things to do. Stupid girls, stay out!"

Trix turned back towards Pippa and shrugged. "Sorry about my little brat, um, I mean brother."

"That box . . ." Pippa started.

"What about it?" Trix asked.

"I-I know that logo on the side," Pippa stammered. "It's from Jake's Joke Shop. My dad ordered a bunch of stuff from there for his best mate's birthday party. It's one of those mail-order places that specialises in practical jokes."

But before Trix could consider all the awful possibilities of partnering her wretched younger brother with a joke shop, the Christmas bells jingled again.

This time Holly called out, "Trix, are you home?"

Trix sprang to her feet and looked around the lounge for any signs of their surprise sleepover. "In here," she called back.

Holly walked slowly into the room. She looked from Trix to Pippa. They both looked as if they'd been caught doing something they shouldn't. Trix tried to act like she usually did but the secret tied her tongue and made her body feel awkward, as if anything she did might give away their top-secret plans.

"I thought I saw you leaving school at the normal time, but you said you were staying late to work on a project." Holly's cheeks were less rosy and her springy red curls less bouncy than usual. Trix and Holly had walked home together almost every day since their very first day of school. Trix couldn't bear the sad look on her best friend's face.

"Um, we were . . ." Pippa started. "We just . . ."

"We finished our project early," Trix lied. She hated doing it. The words felt sticky in her mouth. "Sorry. We should have come to find you." Trix raced to Holly and wrapped her in the biggest hug. She'd been so busy making plans with Pippa for Holly's party that she hadn't considered Holly might be feeling left out.

But she was sure all would be forgiven tomorrow when they surprised Holly with the best sleepover in the history of Little Witching, maybe even the world!

Chapter Three

"Is everyone ready?" Trix shouted as she spun in a slow circle in the middle of her lounge. It was Saturday evening and nearly time for Holly's big birthday surprise. "Chloe, shut those curtains. We don't want Holly to see us. Emma, help Pippa hang the banner."

Trix bounced because her body was overflowing with excitement. It was a big night – a huge night, maybe the biggest and most *huge* night of Trix's life. It was her first birthday surprise sleepover ever, plus she would discover if her best friend was or was not a witch. She would know for sure tonight because she planned to secretly test Holly's magical abilities.

The lounge looked amazing. Chloe and Lucy had arrived early to help hang star shapes cut out of Holly's favourite fashion magazines. They'd also made paper chains from the glossy pages and draped them like bunting from the ceiling. Grace and Sophie had arranged bowls of sweets and salty treats around the room. But Trix was worried.

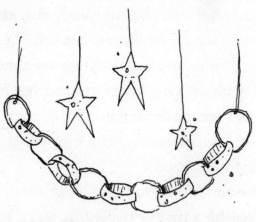

"Everything is going to be fine," Mum assured her as she added chocolate sprinkles to Holly's double-chocolate cake with white chocolate icing.

"Where's Oscar?" Trix asked, remembering the one sure-fire thing that could ruin the party.

"Oscar and your dad left an hour ago," Mum said. "I told you – they're going to the cinema and then staying the night at Granny's."

That should have made Trix feel better but she couldn't forget about Oscar's mysterious box from Jake's Joke Shop. That felt like a bucket of slug-slime and spiders dangling on a rope made of spaghetti right over her head.

"Does everyone remember the plan?" Trix asked, inspecting the goodie bags she and Pippa had assembled that

afternoon. "Holly should be here any minute." Trix and Pippa checked their watches. It was nearly six o'clock.

"We're ready," Pippa said and put her arm around Trix's shoulders. "Lucy's our lookout." Pippa waved at Lucy who was crouched under the front window and peeking through the tiny gap between the curtains. "As soon as we hear the knock on the door, everyone will yell 'Surprise!' Wait, no, first I switch off the lights . . ." Pippa was counting off the steps on her fingers. "When do we use the torches again?"

Trix reviewed the plan for the millionth time. "Knock. Lights out. Open door. Shout 'Surprise!' and flicker our torches at Holly."

Chloe, Lucy, Grace, Sophie and Emma held up their torches, which had been double- and triple-checked.

"What about the confetti?" Pippa asked.

How could Trix have forgotten the confetti? "Throw confetti and *then* flicker lights," she said. She almost couldn't stand it. It was as if the butterflies had escaped from her stomach and were now zooming around her body.

"Someone's coming!" Lucy called.

Pippa dashed to turn off the lights and everyone ducked out of sight, everyone except Trix, who was too overcome with excitement to move. The door knob slowly turned and the door creaked open one centimetre, then two, until . . .

"Surprise!" Trix yelled and two dark figures flashed in the torchlight.

Two figures? One big and one small.

"What are you doing here?" Trix groaned and dragged Dad and Oscar into the lounge.

"Well, that's a fine welcome for your favourite father," Dad said and kissed Trix on the cheek. "I called Holly's mum and made sure Holly hadn't left yet. I wouldn't ruin your surprise."

Dad took Trix aside as Pippa turned the lights back on. "Oscar was feeling sick so we had to come home but, don't worry, we'll stay out of your way."

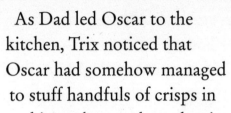

As Dad led Oscar to the
kitchen, Trix noticed that
Oscar had somehow managed
to stuff handfuls of crisps in
his pockets and was leaving
a trail of crumbs behind
him. He didn't seem sick.
Oscar turned when Dad
wasn't looking and stuck
his tongue out at Trix.

He was up to something.
The tiny spot of worry
in the back of Trix's mind grew into a huge,
dark, sleepover-destroying monster!

Chapter Four

Jinx's spots were sparkling. He couldn't help it. Parties were so much fun and to top it all off, this one was going to be a surprise. Jinx loved surprises.

Jinx had tried to stay out of the way, but there were bowls of sweets to inspect and bunting to bat. Being invisible should have made it easier to keep out of the way, but sometimes it made things more difficult.

On Jinx's first day as Trix's familiar, Lulu had cast a special spell to make sure only witches could see and hear Jinx. Trix's dad was allergic to cats so it was the only way Jinx could live with Trix and nobody would be upset. All Jinx had to do was keep away from Dad.

Jinx jumped behind the sofa to avoid being squashed among the girls' shiny shoes. He wished Pippa had brought Twitch but Pippa had asked her lavender rat to stay at home because she knew that some people don't like rats.

Jinx scaled the bookcase. He wanted the best seat in the house for the birthday surprise moment. Watching everyone scurry about below him made Jinx think of ants at a picnic. Dad was trying to coax Oscar out of the kitchen. Trix was giving everyone handfuls of confetti and all the girls were laughing at whatever girls laugh about. Jinx loved the sound of laughter. It was like a tickle to his ears.

A flash of red caught his eye. From this vantage point, he could see through the gap between the curtain rod and the window. A headful of curls was bouncing towards the front door.

Oh, no! Holly was coming and the girls weren't ready. Lucy wasn't at her post so it was up to Jinx to save the surprise!

Meow! Jinx called. Meow! Meow! Meow! This was one of those moments when he wished everyone – not just witches – could see and hear him. Jinx turned his sparkling spots up to their brightest.

Just in time, Trix spotted him. Jinx pointed his paw towards the window and meowed again.

Trix's eyes widened. "Holly's coming!" she shouted.

Knock! Knock! Knock!

Jinx was overwhelmed with excitement. Holly was here!

But then so many things happened at once and all Jinx could do was watch in horror.

Trix dived for the light switch, but so did Pippa. They turned off the lights but knocked heads, which sent them reeling backwards.

Dad sneezed as he passed under Jinx. Dad's sneeze scared Grace who jumped in fright, accidentally flinging her arms into the 'Happy Birthday, Holly!' banner and sending it crashing to the floor. In the dark, the girls bumped into one another, scrambling for their hiding places and torches. Bowls were upturned. As Emma tripped, her handful of confetti fluttered into the air.

Sneaky Oscar made a break for the cake, but Pippa, still stumbling, bumped into him. Oscar was now falling, fingers first, into the cake, which teetered on the edge of the kitchen counter.

"WOLS OM!"

Jinx couldn't believe his ears. It was Trix and she had shouted Lulu's time-altering spell. She shouldn't have done that. New witches weren't supposed to use advanced magic. Jinx wasn't sure Trix's magic would be strong enough. This was a big spell for such a young witch. He wiggled his whiskers to give Trix's new magic a little boost.

Instantly, everything and everyone in the room froze as if zapped by the icy touch of Jack Frost himself – everyone except Trix, Pippa and Jinx who sprang into action.

"We've only got a minute," Trix called. "Pippa, banner. Jinx, cake. I'll tidy."

Jinx leaped over Dad through the frozen confetti. He bounced off the stack of presents and ducked under and sprang over the girls' sprawled arms

and legs as they paused, mid-fall, in the darkened lounge. Crisps and sweets dangled in the air. Jinx snapped at the airborne treats on his way. Salty and sweet tingled on his tongue. This was like the best obstacle course ever.

"Jinx, the cake!" Trix called as she scooped up the floating snacks.

The cake. The cake! Jinx repeated. He must remember his mission. There was no time to spare. But it was so hard to focus when the world seemed topsy-turvy.

Jinx dodged past Pippa, who was re-hanging the banner. Trix was hopping about like a bunny with its tail on fire, putting everything and everyone back into the right places.

Jinx could feel the tug of time speeding up. The cake hovered half-on, half-off, the kitchen counter.

Jinx leaped high into the air. With the tip of his nose he pushed the cake back to safety and gave Oscar a shove on his way down, keeping those greedy fingers away from the cake's fluffy icing.

The silence of frozen time was shattered as the room came back to life. At the front door, Holly's knocking started again.

Everyone looked a bit confused because, for them, the scene had changed in the blink of an eye.

"Everyone ready?" Trix whispered as she made her way to the door.

The knock, knock, knocking on the front door mimicked Jinx's beating heart.

Chapter Five

"SURPRISE!" everyone yelled as Trix threw open the door.

Confetti showered down on Holly and torches flickered on and off like lights at a disco.

"*AAAAHHHHH!*" Holly screamed as she stumbled backwards.

Trix rushed forwards and caught her friend. "Happy birthday, Holly!" Trix talked

fast because she couldn't quite read the
look on Holly's face. Her expression was a
combination of shock and horror. "It's your
very own surprise birthday sleepover party!"

"All this is for me?" Holly asked, spitting
confetti from her lips. "I can't believe it."

Trix thought she could feel time speeding
up to synchronise with the rest of the world.

"Were you surprised?" Pippa asked as she
ushered Holly into the house.

"Yes. Very." Holly replied.

"It's been so difficult keeping the party a

secret," Trix explained. "Pippa and I have been planning it for weeks."

Holly hugged Trix and Pippa in a too-tight hug. "So that's what you've been doing." Trix tried to wiggle free but Holly kept right on hugging. "I thought, well, you'll think I'm so silly now, but I was feeling left out. I knew there was something going on but I never guessed . . ." Holly took a big breath and then declared, "No more secrets, ever!"

Trix felt a tiny pang of guilt in her tummy. She was still keeping a secret from Holly – the biggest and most important secret of her life. She wished she could tell Holly that she was a witch, but that would break the Sisterhood of Magic's number one rule – never tell anyone that you're a witch. But if Holly was a witch too then there would be no more secrets between them. Trix wished and hoped and prayed that Holly had the gift of magic. She crossed her fingers and toes and even whispered "Abracadabra" for extra luck.

"Happy birthday, weirdo," Oscar said and

bumped into the three-way hug. "Girls are so stupid."

Holly grabbed Oscar and kissed him on the forehead. "Thanks, Oscar!"

"Aw, gross!" Oscar rubbed his forehead and quickly thudded upstairs.

"That should keep him away for the rest of the evening," Trix said with a laugh.

The rest of the girls rushed over to greet Holly. Trix switched on the lights. Her smile stretched as wide as it would go. It was nice to see Holly surrounded by so many friends. Until recently Holly had been the shyest girl at Little Witching Primary.

Psst! Pippa crooked her finger at Trix and nodded towards the kitchen.

"What's the matter?" Trix whispered to Pippa when they were huddled in the farthest corner of the room.

"We aren't supposed to use advanced magic!" Pippa hissed, looking around to make sure no one was listening. Luckily, Mum was ushering Dad upstairs to keep an eye on Oscar and the girls were giving Holly her gifts.

Trix shrugged. "I didn't mean to. It just sort of happened." The spell had popped into her head and out of her mouth. And everything seemed normal now – well, as normal as anything ever seemed in her house.

"I understand," Pippa said, nodding. "I didn't mean to last week, but I accidentally filled my dad's shoes with sweets. I was trying to find a spell for non-stinky shoes and I rhymed *sweet* and *feet*. Then I had to explain why Dad's trainers were filled with Smarties!" Pippa frowned. "Shame to ruin all that chocolate. Anyway, what was I saying?" Pippa squinted as if she was thinking harder. "Oh, yes. No more magic. OK, Trix?"

Trix nodded.

"You could get into big trouble for using advanced magic. It messes with the space and time whatsit Lulu mentioned. And we both want to be fairy godmothers some day, don't we?" Pippa added.

Trix nodded again. She wanted that more than anything. Well, she wanted her best friend Holly to be a witch first and *then* she wanted to be a fairy godmother second. She also wanted it to rain chocolate – just once – and her brother not to be so mean all the time. And then there was also her secret desire to own the first sweetshop on the moon . . .

"Trix?" Pippa was staring at her, and Trix realised that her brain had switched to daydream mode.

"What?" Trix asked and concentrated really hard on Pippa and not her dream of selling marshmallows to Martians.

"Promise me," Pippa said.

Trix had definitely missed something. "Promise you what?"

"No more magic tonight," Pippa said. "I don't want you to get into trouble." Trix had never seen Pippa look more serious.

Trix thought for a second. She didn't want to lie, so she chose her words carefully. "I'll be good." She couldn't promise not to use magic again tonight because she *did* plan to use it. She had to find out once and for all if Holly was a witch – and to do that she was going to need a little sneaky magic.

Chapter Six

"What is it?" Holly asked, turning the present over and over in her hands. It was a bit bigger than a shoe box and wrapped with special birthday paper, ten silvery bows and lots and lots of twirly ribbons. "I'm sure I'll love it."

Trix bounced on the sofa next to Holly, a pile of crumpled wrapping paper at her feet. She'd found the most perfect birthday present for Holly. Trix wriggled her toes and made the wrapping paper dance. She was nearly as excited about giving the present as Holly was about getting it.

Kersplat!

Out of nowhere Jinx leaped into the middle of the paper, sending bows and ribbons flying in every direction. Trix quickly kicked her feet among the wrapping to disguise the antics of her invisible kitten.

"Oh, Trix, it's perfect!" Holly giggle-snorted as she ripped the last of the paper

away and opened the box. She held up the white-tipped black cane she found inside. "I know what this is. It's a deluxe magic kit!" She waved the wand over the pile of wrapping paper just as Jinx dived underneath it again. "Abracafizzle!" The papers and bows sprang into the air.

The girls squealed. "Do it again!"

"Did I do that?" Holly asked, inspecting the wand.

"Oops!" Trix said and gave the papers and Jinx a gentle nudge. "That was me." Jinx scampered off among the girls, who were sitting cross-legged around Holly. Even though Jinx was invisible, keeping him hidden at a sleepover was turning out to be more difficult than holding a sandcastle or hugging butterflies or saving ice lollies under her pillow – and Trix had tried and failed at all those things.

The time had come for Trix's first test of Holly's magical abilities. "Why don't you show everyone a trick?" Trix asked Holly. "You're a great magician."

Holly blushed and slouched back into the sofa. "I don't know."

"Something simple – like the vanishing coin." Trix handed her a little box and a pound coin. "I wrote you a spell – I mean a magical rhyme – to say when you do the trick." She pulled a note out of her pocket.

Pippa gave Trix a look that said she knew Trix was up to something. But it didn't matter, because in a few minutes Trix would know for certain that Holly was a witch and everything would be perfect. "Just give it a go, Holly."

Holly put the coin inside the box, making sure that everyone could see it there. Then she closed the lid and read Trix's spell. "Little coin, I am sincere," Holly muttered in the super-quiet voice she usually saved for secrets. "I want to see you disappear."

That was the spell Trix had used to make a coin disappear at one of her first lessons with Lulu. It had to work for Holly. It just had to.

Holly waved the wand over the box and tapped it one, two, three times. Trix twisted her arms behind her back and crossed her fingers. She crossed her legs and crossed her toes.

Holly's lips curled into a cheeky smile as she slowly opened the box. Trix held her breath.

The coin was gone!

Vanished!

Disappeared!

The girls clapped and Trix punched the air and whooped. The other girls gave Trix a funny look. The trick was good, but Trix realised her reaction seemed a bit extreme. The girls didn't understand that this was the best news ever. Even better than when Trix had found a five-pound note on the high street or when Oscar had been snowed in at their grandparents' house for two extra days! It was almost as good as the moment when Jinx had picked Trix as his witch.

Jinx! Why hadn't Trix thought of him before? If Holly was a witch, then she should now be able to see Jinx. Holly would love him and, of course, she'd soon get her own familiar. Trix's mind raced as she wondered what kind of familiar Holly would have and thought about all the magical things they could do together.

"You are the world's best wi— magician." Trix corrected her almost huge mistake.

"It was nothing," Holly said, revealing the secret compartment in the box and the missing coin.

Trix blinked and blinked again. The coin had un-vanished.

"I saw this trick on YouTube, but I've never had the chance to practise it in real life before," Holly said. She did the trick again without reciting Trix's spell and the coin disappeared.

Trix sighed. She was going to have to find another way to tell whether Holly was a witch.

"I've got another magic trick I want all of you to do," Mum called from the kitchen. "Help me make this pizza disappear!"

Holly hugged Trix again. "Thanks for the best present and the best birthday ever. We will be best friends until we grow grey hair, wear sensible shoes and smell funny!"

Everyone but Trix raced into the kitchen. Trix looked at the coin and then at Holly, who was already devouring a piece of pizza. There was no doubt that Holly was the best friend in the world, but was she, or was she not, a witch?

Chapter Seven

Jinx pushed open the door to Trix's bedroom. He'd had enough of surprise parties. There were too many rules. He was supposed to stay away from Dad because he was allergic to cats and Jinx didn't like making anyone unhappy or sneezy. He was supposed to stay hidden and quiet, but the wrapping paper was so sparkly and the bows so pretty. He loved the sound of the crinkling paper. That sound made his paws dance and his ears hum.

There was something about paper that begged to be pounced on and made it practically impossible to stay out of the way. But now he was ready for a snooze.

He made his body as skinny as he could and squeezed through the now partially open door. He'd hide out in here until bedtime. Dad had moved Trix's bed into Oscar's room, and Trix and Pippa had arranged dozens of blankets and pillows on the floor to create one fun fluffy bed.

Trix's twenty-three cat toys were scattered around. Jinx greeted each one with a touch of his nose or a flick of his tail. He imagined he was king of

the cats in Trixland. He tumbled with one cat and danced with another. He loved playing make-believe! In his imagination, he could be whatever he wanted.

Super Jinx!

He swooped under one of the blankets and rolled until he was tucked into a nice snuggly cocoon. He wriggled until the tip of his nose and one eye found an opening. He was Jinx the spy cat, keeping watch over the sleepover to guard it from evil party-wreckers . . .

Creeeeeak.

Trix's door was opening slowly.

Jinx tried to stay very still. That's what good spies did. Jinx wasn't good at keeping still. His nose twitched. His ears itched. His tail squirmed. But he waited and watched.

A small dark figure ducked inside the room and eased the door closed. Jinx's ears pricked up. His fur fluffed. He was ready to defend Trixland! Jinx focused his laser-like spy vision on the intruder.

He immediately recognised his enemy. He'd know that messy hair and chocolate-smudged face anywhere. It was the dreaded little BOTHER, Oscar.

What is Oscar doing in Trix's room? Jinx wondered. Trix's room was off limits to pesky little brothers.

Oscar removed a container he'd been concealing under his shirt. "A few shakes of this and there won't be any sleeping tonight." Oscar sniggered to himself.

What was Oscar up to? Jinx knew Oscar was a number-one pest. He'd put bugs in Trix's fairy cakes. He'd even ripped out the last two pages of the book Trix was reading so she wouldn't know how the story ended. Oscar seemed to only have fun when he was making Trix's life miserable.

Well, not on my watch! Jinx vowed.

One of the wonderful things about being invisible was the ability to sneak and creep. Jinx crawled closer to Oscar.

Oscar shook what looked like powder onto the blankets. Jinx sniffed at the power and sneezed.

Some of the powder blew onto Oscar's foot. He immediately started scratching. "This stuff works!" Oscar looked at the container and shook the rest of it over the pillows. He scratched his foot again and again. "This is going to be great!"

Jinx understood. Itching powder. Oscar had
sprinkled itching powder all over Trix's room. If
Jinx didn't do something, it would be more of a
scratch-over than a sleepover.

Oscar had just turned to leave when he spotted
Trix's iPod and the carrier bag of sweets Trix had
saved for a midnight feast.

Oh, no!

Oscar tucked the bag of sweets under his arm. "A snack for later. Thank you, Trix," he whispered. Then he grabbed Trix's iPod and pushed a few buttons. "Holly's birthday playlist. How do I delete it?" Oscar was just fumbling with the buttons when they both heard the thud of feet on the stairs.

Oscar froze. Someone was coming. He tiptoed to the door. So did Jinx. He peeped out. So did Jinx. It was Dad.

Just then Jinx thought of a brilliant spy plan.

He hissed and pounced on Oscar's feet.

"Aaaaahhhh!" Oscar screamed, dropping the bag of sweets and Trix's iPod. He bolted out of the door and right into Dad.

"What were you doing in Trix's room?" Dad asked, but his tone said he knew Oscar had been up to no good. "I think you need to go to your room. You're obviously feeling well enough to clean it, and tomorrow I think you will help Trix clean up after the party, too!"

"Aw, Dad," Oscar whined, but he had been caught red-handed – or itchy-footed.

Jinx may have saved the sweets and the party

music, but he still had one big, scratchy problem to sort out. How was he going to tell Trix about the itching powder?

Chapter Eight

Ten pink candles glowed on top of Holly's birthday cake. The girls had gathered around the kitchen table and were singing *Happy Birthday* to Holly, who was beaming brighter than the candles.

"Make a wish," Mum prompted.

Holly puffed out her cheeks and screwed her eyes shut tightly.

Trix wondered what Holly was wishing

for. She knew the wish she wanted to come true tonight. *Please, please, pretty please with sugar and chocolate and sprinkles on the top! Please let Holly be a witch!*

Holly blew out her candles in one sweeping blow. The girls cheered.

"Now your wish will come true!" Chloe said.

"What did you wish for?" Lucy asked.

"She can't tell you or it won't come true," Trix said quickly. Wishes were an important business. She loved the idea of granting people's wishes when she became a fairy godmother.

"I don't mind telling," Holly said and swiped a fingerful of icing. "I was going to wish that we'd have the best sleepover ever, but then I realised . . ." she draped one arm around Trix and the other around Pippa, "that my wish has already come true, thanks to the two of you!"

"Mum, is it OK if we go up to my room and listen to music?" Trix asked when the last bite of chocolate cake had been washed down with the last sip of fizzy lemonade. "I made a playlist on my iPod of your favourite music," Trix told Holly.

"Oh, that sounds great!" Holly said. "You've thought of everything."

"Don't play the music too loudly and

wake your brother," Mum said as she stacked the dirty dishes. "Have fun!"

Trix led the girls through the lounge and up the stairs to her room. Oscar's door was open a crack and Trix could swear she saw his shifty eyeball peering through the opening.

What is Oscar up to? Her little brother was going to try and ruin her first sleepover. She could feel it her bones.

She stopped in her tracks. Holly ran right into her and the rest of the girls skidded to a stop.

"What are you doing?" Holly asked and rubbed her crunched nose.

But Trix couldn't say. Her invisible kitten was pacing back and forth in front of Trix's bedroom door as if he were guarding it. He stopped and sat up on his hind legs. Trix raised her eyebrows to ask what was wrong. She hoped her connection with Jinx was working.

Jinx pointed a paw towards Oscar's door. Then Jinx scratched his ear and his neck and his side. He practically tied himself in knots, scratching.

Oscar and scratching?

She wasn't very good at charades.

Holly nudged Trix. "Look!"

Have Holly's magical abilities kicked in? Can she see Jinx too? Trix wondered.

But Holly was looking in the opposite direction. She nodded towards Oscar's room. Trix glanced over in time to see Oscar's door shut quickly.

"Holly . . ." Trix pointed to where Jinx had been a moment ago. If Holly could see Jinx then she must be a witch! But Jinx had vanished. "Never mind," Trix sighed.

"I think Oscar is up to something," Holly told Trix.

"Me too," Trix said. "Gather round."

The girls huddled up like they were in a rugby scrum. "I have a bad feeling that my little brother Oscar has played some sort of trick on us. It's time to show him that little brothers and sleepovers don't mix."

The girls nodded as Trix explained her plan.

"Oscar," Holly called through the door, "are you asleep?"

"Go away!" Oscar yelled.

"There's an extra piece of my birthday cake and I thought you might like—" But before Holly could even finish her offer, Oscar was out of his room and racing down to the kitchen.

"Lucy and Chloe, you watch him," Trix instructed. The two girls nodded and followed Oscar downstairs. "Emma, Sophie and Grace, you stand guard."

The girls posted themselves at the top, bottom and middle of the staircase.

"This is like a film I saw on TV," Pippa

said. "We're like detectives looking for clues. It's so exciting." She giggled as she, Trix and Holly slipped into Oscar's room.

They searched high and low.

"I've got it!" Holly said, pulling an orange box from under Oscar's bed. "Not the cleverest of hiding places."

"Creeping cats!" Trix said when she opened the box and saw the empty container labelled *Itching Powder*. That had been what Jinx was trying to tell her. Oscar must have sprinkled itching powder on their big sleepover bed.

"Let's give Oscar an itch of his own scratching!" Trix said.

Holly and Pippa swapped Oscar's blanket for one of the ones he'd coated in itching powder. "Be careful and wash your hands when you're finished," Trix said. "I'll take care of the rest of this stuff."

Trix went into her room and shut the door. She needed a rhyme. "*Times like these I'm glad I'm a witch*," Trix started her rhyme, and Jinx appeared next to her, wiggling his whiskers to give Trix's spell a little more power. "*Now make things clean so we don't itch!*" The blankets and pillows fluffed themselves, and a white powder wafted into the air and disappeared in a shimmer of light.

Trix heard the familiar *thump*, *thump*, *thump* of Oscar charging up the stairs.

"You yucky girls, get out of my way," Trix heard him shout, followed swiftly by the sound of his bedroom door slamming.

The girls came racing into Trix's bedroom. Trix hoped her spell had countered the itching powder. They'd know soon enough. The girls collapsed into the pile of cushions and covers.

"I feel like dancing!" Holly said, switching on the iPod and attaching its speakers. Her favourite song started to play.

AAAAGH!

Even over the music, Trix heard Oscar's yell. She opened the door and peered out. Jinx peeked out too. Oscar was in the hallway and he looked as if he were dancing to the music. But he wasn't. He was scratching himself all over.

Jinx looked up and winked at Trix.

Yes, Trix thought, *we do make a good team!*

Her sleepover was saved and Oscar was learning an important lesson – you don't mess with a witch!

Chapter Nine

The long black tail of Trix's cat clock swished from side to side. The girls sat in a circle in the middle of Trix's room. Jinx had disappeared – Trix guessed he'd found a cosy, quiet spot for a catnap. The clock's big and little hands clicked into position, both pointing straight up, and the clock started to meow.

Midnight!

"What should we do now?" Holly asked, her eyes still bright with happiness.

"I'm getting sleepy," Chloe said as she rested her head on a nearby pillow.

"We can't go to bed yet," Trix said. She had thought of one more test to see if Holly was a witch.

"It *is* called a sleepover," Lucy murmured and slipped down next to Chloe.

"Let's go outside and tell ghost stories!" Trix jumped up, pulling Pippa to her feet.

"What? Huh?" Pippa yawned. "I vote for sleep."

"Not yet, Pippa," Trix begged. "Let's sneak out. It will be fun."

"I don't know . . ." Holly looked outside at the full moon glowing in the dark sky. "Full moons are kind of creepy."

"Full moons are magical!" Trix exclaimed. She had discovered she was a witch when she'd seen Lulu and her cat familiar, Sparkles, flying across the full moon at midnight on Trix's tenth birthday. If Lulu took another midnight flight tonight, maybe Holly would see her and then Trix would know for sure that Holly was a witch!

Trix grabbed Holly's hand and led the way down the stairs. A bleary-eyed train of girls in pyjamas followed, gradually waking up as excitement took hold. They tiptoed through the lounge, but the harder they tried to be quiet, the louder they seemed to be. Lucy stubbed her toe on the sofa. Emma slipped on the confetti. And soon all the girls were giggling at their midnight parade.

If they woke Mum and Dad, Trix knew she'd be in big trouble. "Shhhh!" she hissed as they reached the back door.

The girls gathered round as Trix slowly unlocked the door and eased it open.

"Oh, this is so exciting," Pippa said, racing ahead into the garden. "I feel like we're secret agents!"

All the girls followed.

"I've never been out at midnight before," Holly said with a giggle-snort of laughter.

The girls spun around barefooted in the dew-kissed grass. The cool night air raised goose bumps on Trix's arms. The night felt so silent – it was as if the rest of the world were holding its breath, waiting to see if Holly was a witch.

The bright full moon seemed to focus like a spotlight on Trix's friends and make the trees and flowers glow all around them. Trix froze this image in her mind. No matter what happened, she'd remember this moment when her friends fluttered like fairies in the midnight moonlight.

Suddenly, the night sky seemed to soften to a smoky blue and the moon looked like a million diamonds glued together into one big, beautiful ball. Gliding across the moon was the silhouette of Lulu in her pointy witch's hat and flowing gown, with Sparkles perched on the bushy back of her besom.

Trix remembered her moonlit flight with Aunt Belle over London. She wondered if she and Jinx had looked so spectacular. She had felt scared, surprised and happy all jumbled together. Oh, how she hoped Holly would get to feel that way some day!

But, right now, she needed to find out if Holly could see Lulu. That should be easy. "Look at the moon," Trix said and pointed with crossed fingers right at Lulu.

"Payback time!" Oscar called from the back door. He scratched his elbow. He scratched his leg. "I hope you like the cold and the dark because I'm locking you out!" With one more scratch, he slammed the door.

The girls lunged for the handle but it was too late. They heard the thud as the lock clicked into place.

Now what are we going to do? Trix wondered. If they woke Mum and Dad, they'd be in big trouble. If they woke the neighbours, they'd be in *double* trouble.

Trix was trying to think of a word that rhymed with *unlock* when the door sprang

open. Mum appeared in the doorway. She had
hedgehog hair and a sleep-wrinkled face. She
was wearing her fuzzy blue dressing gown
and matching slippers. "To bed! All of you!"
Mum turned and pointed at Oscar who was
hiding under the kitchen table. "That means
you too, Oscar!"

"Sorry, Mum," Trix said. Mum smiled a
sleepy smile but her eyes said that they'd be
talking about this tomorrow.

"Do you think if we called them wake-overs

we'd get more sleep?" Pippa asked as she passed Mum.

Mum ruffled Pippa's sagging ponytail. "Good question, my dear."

Trix turned Holly back towards the moon and pointed. "Holly, don't you see . . ." But Lulu and Sparkles had disappeared – like Trix's hope of proving that Holly was a witch.

Chapter Ten

Jinx chased Twitch, Tabby and Rascal around the cauldron while Sherlock circled above. It was good to see his familiar friends again. Maybe he'd have a familiar sleepover on his birthday.

"I love Mondays," Lulu sang as she twirled around the magic classroom, dodging two cats, a rat, a pug, an owl and five young witches-in-training. "It's like a fresh start full of hope and promise. This week we will continue with our lesson on potions. What did we learn last week?"

"I learned that Trix is a klutz," Stella muttered as the girls took their places around the table in the middle of the room.

Stella was so mean. Last Friday Jinx had seen Stella intentionally bump into Trix, which had caused her to slip and nearly bring the bookcase full of magical ingredients crashing down. Jinx leaped on the table in front of Stella and flicked his tail right in her face to let her know what he thought of her.

Stella batted Jinx away.

"Stella, did you have an answer for me?" Lulu asked. Everyone looked at Stella.

"Um, no, I mean it was Trix's silly familiar, he jumped—" Stella blushed a little and Jinx thought the rosy colour in her cheeks would be the perfect ingredient for a glow-in-the-dark potion. He wished he could make potions. He'd make a giggle potion and a snoozy potion and a potion that would make things sparkle like his spots.

"Oh, I know!" Pippa raised her hand and kept pumping it higher in the air. "Pick me! I know!"

Jinx liked Pippa. If Pippa was a potion, she would be made of sunbeams and honeysuckle and marshmallows.

"Something tells me that Pippa has the answer," Lulu said and gestured in Pippa's direction, which set her bangles to jingle-jangling.

Jinx loved the sound of Lulu's bracelets. They seemed to ring a sweet little tune of their own. That was the sound of magic – because, whenever Lulu was around, something magical always happened.

Oh! Jinx had missed Pippa's answer, but it was probably something about potions lasting longer than spells. He already knew that. He also knew that witches could make age-old potions from recipes that had been handed down from one witchy generation to the next, or they could invent their own potions.

"I taught you a few classic potions last week." Lulu flicked her wrist and clicked her fingers and mixing bowls appeared in front of each witch. "Today I want you to create your own Happy Potion. Every fairy godmother needs a Happy Potion." With another flick of her bangle-filled wrist, a line of test tubes with cork stoppers appeared in front of Lulu. "Sometimes people need

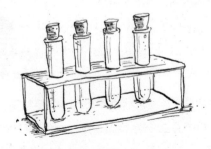

a drop or two to help them find their happiness – which can get buried under a lot of silly everyday worries." Lulu lifted a silver chain from around her neck. On the end of the chain was a tiny glass jar. "This is my Happy Potion." She was standing behind Stella now. "My potion includes things that make me happy, like the twinkle of the stars on a midnight ride, the colour of my nephew's eyes and the crackle from the spine of a new book."

"How can we possibly collect things like crackles and twinkles?" Stella asked in the snotty tone she usually reserved for Trix.

"You're a witch," Lulu said. "Use your magical imagination!" She clapped her hands. "OK, my lovely witches, start thinking happy. You can use any ingredients from my collection but try to make up some of your own."

Jinx never needed a Happy Potion. He made his own brand of happy. But if he were making a Happy Potion, he'd include shimmer from a rainbow, all the colours of butterflies' wings, and the sound of Trix's laughter.

Jinx scampered over to Trix's side. His whiskers were ready to wiggle if she needed any help. He blinked his bright golden eyes up at Trix.

Trix combed her fingers through Jinx's fur. "My Happy Potion will contain a touch of Jinx's sparkle," Trix said and rubbed the cat hair from her fingers into her mixing bowl.

Jinx purred louder and sparkled brighter. He

loved that he made Trix happy. Jinx tumbled on the table, accidentally knocking into a few test tubes.

"What else should I include?" Trix asked Jinx. Jinx had a great idea. He scratched his head to rumple his fur, plucked a whisker from his nose, waved the whisker like a magic wand and did his best Holly impression.

Trix kissed him on the nose. "That's exactly right. Holly always makes me happy."

Jinx pointed a paw at Trix's blazer. A strand of Holly's hair was stuck there. Trix placed the hair in the mixing bowl with Jinx's fur. "I think we need something to mush it all together. I'll be right back." Trix went over to study Lulu's amazing collection of witchy ingredients.

Stella must have thought Jinx wasn't looking because she immediately sprinkled some powder into Trix's bowl and then quickly put the container back on the bottom shelf of the bookcase. Jinx rushed over to see what it was. The jar was black. Jinx placed his front paws on the jar to take a closer look. There was writing on the label, but he couldn't read.

"Oh, you don't want any of that," Lulu said and scooped Jinx into her arms. "That's the dark of the darkest night!"

Jinx had to tell Lulu that Stella had poured some of that awful stuff into Trix's potion. He opened his mouth to meow when the air was suddenly filled with the most awful sound. It was like a combination of a howl and a bark and a scary laugh.

"Magic marbles!" Lulu placed Jinx on the table. "Someone has opened the laugh of the hyena. An easy mistake to make." Lulu dashed off to help Cara and Becka, who were struggling to replace the lid on the container that was bouncing around the table top.

Jinx flattened himself and covered his ears with his paws. That sound actually hurt. Through squinted eyes, he saw Trix mixing something into her potion, then pouring it all into a test tube and tucking it into her blazer pocket.

Lulu was busy wrestling the howling container to the floor. "Class dismissed," Lulu shouted. "I need to sprinkle a little 'quiet as a mouse' in here but it will take a while to clear the sound. Keep thinking about your potions and I'll see you tomorrow!"

Jinx followed Trix into the quiet of the library. All that noise had jumbled his brain. There was something important he needed to tell Trix but, for the life of him, he couldn't remember what it was.

Chapter Eleven

"Can I try one?" Trix begged the next day when Holly showed her the edible assignment she'd made for her Cookery class. The box was full of round, bumpy balls with the unmistakable look and smell of chocolate. Even before Trix knew she was a witch, chocolate had made her believe in magic.

"Just one," Holly said, handing Trix a

chocolatey circle. "I have to save enough for everyone in my Cookery class."

Trix placed the treat in her mouth. The chocolate was crunchy on the outside and smooth on the inside, and it had a hint of mint. "These are magically amazing! What do you call them?"

"I haven't come up with a name yet," Holly said. "But how about Mint Magic?"

"That's a perfect . . ." Trix lost her train of thought as she spotted Jinx bounding down the corridor. She was still surprised every time she saw her familiar show up whenever and wherever he wanted.

"Are you OK, Trix?" Holly asked, giving her friend a playful nudge.

"Yeah, fine," Trix said as Jinx skidded to a stop right by her trainers. Oh, how she wished Holly knew about Jinx! But if Holly were a witch, she would certainly comment on the adorable kitten who was now batting at Trix's shoelaces. Trix had pretty much given up on Holly being a witch. A tiny part of her still hoped that maybe Holly's magical abilities were just delayed, like trains and buses – or Aunt Belle's birthday cards when she was somewhere far, far away – but deep down Trix knew it wasn't very likely.

"What are you doing in Arts and Crafts?" Holly asked as the pair started to walk towards their final class of the day.

Without thinking, Trix removed the test tube from her blazer pocket. "We are making po—" Trix stopped abruptly when she noticed Jinx shaking his head. What was she doing? She couldn't tell Holly she'd made her very own Happy Potion. She tried to recover. "I've made organic paint. You know, paint out of everyday stuff."

Holly crinkled her nose at the dark liquid sloshing in Trix's tube. "I'm sorry you got stuck in Arts and Crafts with Stella."

"It's not so bad," Trix said as they arrived at the stairway that led to the library. "Lulu is really fun, and that's how I met Pippa."

"See you after school," Holly said but she suddenly looked a little sad.

"What's the matter?" Trix asked.

Holly shrugged. "I like Cookery but I wish I could be with you and Pippa. It would be more fun with friends."

Then Trix had a genius idea. She would try her Happy Potion on Holly. It couldn't hurt, right? Her best friend definitely looked like she could use a little dose of happiness. When Holly turned to go, Trix quickly uncorked her test tube and tipped a drop of her potion onto Holly's head. She expected to hear Holly's giggle-snort of laughter. But that's not what happened. That's not what happened at all.

As Holly walked away, Trix watched her best friend vanish into thin air.

Creeping cats!

Trix could only think of two options. Either Holly had somehow found her magic or Trix's Happy Potion had gone terribly wrong.

"Um, Holly . . ." Trix started, hoping that her friend was only invisible and not transported somewhere else or transformed into a speck of dust or suffering from some other terrible magical effect.

Holly's box of Mint Magic was floating
down the hall. "Holly, wait up!" Trix raced
over to her best friend. Sophie was coming
along the corridor and Trix didn't want her
to wonder why a box of Mint Magic was
floating down the hallway by itself!

"Hi, Sophie!" Holly called as her friend
passed by.

Trix grabbed for the floating box of
chocolates.

"Hey!" Holly said and hung on to the

box so that it seemed to bounce in the air.

"Hi, Trix!" Sophie called and gave Trix a funny look because Trix appeared to be waving the box around wildly.

Trix awkwardly put her arm around what she thought was Holly's middle. "You've got to come with me," she whispered and tried to lead invisible Holly towards the stairs.

"Why didn't Sophie say hi to me?" Holly's voice was sad again. "I thought we were friends."

"You *are* friends. It's not that. It's just . . ." Trix's voice trailed away. She didn't know how to tell her friend that she was invisible. "You've *really* got to come with me."

Holly tried to pull away. "I can't be late to class."

"Holly, you've got to trust me," Trix said and Holly stopped struggling.

"What's the matter?" she asked, a tremor in her voice.

"Follow me." Trix led Holly to the library. "It's going to be OK." She said it but, at that moment, she didn't believe it. She had no idea what to do, but she knew she couldn't keep Holly's invisibility a secret for much longer.

Chapter Twelve

Trix wished she could see the expression on Holly's face, but Trix couldn't see any part of Holly. She was still completely invisible. At least now they were at the very back of the library where no one could see – or *not* see – them.

"That's not funny," Holly said. She'd jerked free of Trix's grasp the moment Trix had finished explaining that she was invisible.

"It's no joke," Trix said, spinning around in a slow circle, trying to figure out exactly where her best friend was.

"That's not possible. I can't be invisible. But . . . but . . . I can't see my own hands or legs or . . ."

Trix wished her Happy Potion actually worked because Holly was sounding scared.

"Trix, what's happening to me?" Holly asked.

"Come here, Holly. I've got an idea." Trix puffed up her cheeks and, when Holly bumped into her, she blew as hard as she could at the dusty books on the library shelves.

Atchoo! Holly sneezed, but Trix's idea had worked. A dusty film now coated Holly and Trix could see the outline of her friend.

"What's that?" Holly pointed to Jinx who was now also covered in dust.

"That's Jinx. He's my invisible familiar, and I'm a witch," Trix said, as simply as if she were saying 'I'm hungry'. Trix caught Holly as she began to slowly slide down the bookcase.

Sitting on the library floor, Trix calmly told Holly everything. She started with how she'd seen Lulu's midnight ride across the moon on her tenth birthday, continued with her invisible familiar and finished with her obviously messed-up Happy Potion.

Jinx rubbed up against Holly's leg.

"It's nice to meet you, Jinx," Holly said and gave Jinx a stroke, accidentally brushing most of the dust off him. "I knew you were keeping secrets from me, Trix."

"I couldn't tell you. It's the first rule of the

Sisterhood of Magic. I'm going to be in big trouble for making you invisible and telling you everything, but you're my best friend and . . ."

The shrill sound of laughter rang out through the library – not just any laughter, either. Trix recognised the awful sound of Stella's voice. "Creeping cats!" Trix said and brushed the dust off Holly. "Stella can't know you're here. I'll think of something, I promise." The girls sprang to their feet, and Trix swept Holly behind her.

"What's wrong with you now?" Stella asked as she pushed past Trix. "Did you forget how to get into the magic classroom?" Stella and Cara walked right up to the bookcase. It fizzled and transformed into the big wooden door that led to the hidden room.

Holly gasped.

So Trix gasped to cover up Holly's surprise.

"Why does she always act so weird?" Stella said to Cara. "People like her give witches a bad name."

"She's horrible," Holly whispered from somewhere near Trix's ear.

Trix nodded.

"Hi, Trix!" Pippa called as she entered the library. "Were you waiting for me?"

"Oh, Pippa, there's something I need to tell you." Trix rushed over to Pippa. Maybe she would know what to do, but would telling Pippa only get her into trouble too? Questions were exploding in Trix's brain like fireworks, making it hard for her to think.

"What's wrong?" Pippa asked.

Trix looked over to where she thought Holly was standing and then to the flickering door and then to Stella and Cara. What was the right thing to do?

"Hurry along, my little witches!" Lulu called from inside the magic classroom. "Don't waste time unless you can make it!"

Trix gulped. *Making time.* Lulu's words reminded Trix that she had used advanced magic to slow down time to save Holly's surprise party. She wondered if there was advanced magic that could make Holly reappear.

"You better get going," Stella said in her most snarky tone.

"Aren't you coming?" Trix asked. The only thing worse than leaving Holly behind was leaving her *with Stella*.

"I'm waiting for Becka," Stella said and flipped her perfectly straightened hair over her shoulder, "but you'd better go because you need all the help you can get."

Trix saw a book slip from the shelf and bonk Stella right on the head.

"Ouch!" Stella said, rubbing her head. "How did you do that?" Stella pointed her finger right at Trix's face.

"*I* didn't do anything," Trix said and tried really hard not to smile. Maybe having an invisible friend wasn't so bad after all. Trix secretly winked at Holly and whispered, "Stay here. I'll think of something."

Trix followed Pippa into the magic classroom. What else could she do? She didn't want to act suspiciously. She hoped that with more time she'd be able to figure out a way to help her best friend without getting expelled from the Sisterhood of Magic.

Chapter Thirteen

Jinx bounced between invisible Holly and the door to the magic classroom. He didn't know what to do. He wanted to follow Trix inside but something told him that he should stay with Holly. Jinx slipped out of sight under one of the library's reading tables. Stella was acting more strangely than usual, her gaze darting around the library as if she were making sure no one was around.

He tiptoed over and nudged Holly's leg. She reached down and stroked him.

"She's up to something," Holly whispered to Jinx. He nodded. He thought so, too.

Just then, Becka burst into the library and rushed over to Stella and Cara.

"Did you get it?" Stella asked in a hushed whisper.

Becka nodded. "It wasn't easy, but I got all the ingredients. The powder from a crushed mirror was the toughest to find." Becka held up a glowing test tube and carefully removed the cork from the top.

"What's that?" Holly crouched down next to Jinx. He shook his whole body in response. He wished he knew.

"I borrowed the rest of the stuff from my grandmama," Stella said. "Her collection of ingredients is almost as extensive as Lulu's. She doesn't know what I'm making." Stella pulled two tiny bags from her pocket and dumped the contents into the tube. "Wart shavings from a hog's bottom and slime from a shell-less snail." Then she snatched the tube from Becka's hand, put the cork back in and shook it up. The contents turned the most awful shade of green and the smell of rotten eggs filled the library.

"That's it! We've done it." Stella laughed an evil laugh. "An Ugly Potion. I can't wait to see what this will do to Trix."

Jinx shuddered.

Holly gasped.

"What was that?" Stella turned towards Holly. "Is someone there?"

Jinx curled himself in a tight ball.

"We don't want to be late," Cara said and looped one arm through Stella's and the other through Becka's.

"Drat and double drat!" Holly said when the girls had slipped through the door into the magic classroom. "We can't let that nasty girl make Trix ugly."

Jinx's eyes twinkled with a terribly clever idea. He wiggled his whiskers and turned up the sparkle in his spots to maximum brightness.

"Oh!" Holly exclaimed as a glowing outline of Jinx came into focus. "How did you do that?"

Jinx waved his paw towards the door that was now flickering and fading back into a bookcase, and they both darted inside as the door creaked closed.

Jinx could hear Holly's stifled squeals. He'd forgotten how extraordinary the magic classroom was. Lulu stood at the cauldron in the centre. Red and blue smoke was billowing from the bubbling pot, creating ribbons of purple in the air above.

Holly leaned down next to Jinx and whispered. "Is that Lulu?"

Jinx nodded. Lulu looked perfectly magical when she transformed into her witchy regalia. A pointy black hat topped her long silver curls. Her black gown shimmered with sequins. Until now, Holly had only seen Lulu in her frumpy librarian disguise.

"We've got to warn Trix," Holly told Jinx.

Normally he would tell Lulu about Stella's nasty plans, but he'd brought a non-witch into one of the most top-secret places of all. A non-witch that his witch had turned invisible! He was supposed to look out for Trix, which wasn't always the easiest job. She was the kindest, nicest witch, but trouble had a way of finding her.

Jinx's tail stood straight up. The tip twitched with the thought of his brilliant idea. He would save Trix and give Stella a taste of her own ugliness.

Jinx knocked his head against Holly, and she gave him a stroke. He nudged her towards Trix. He hoped she understood what he was trying to tell her.

Jinx the spy cat was back, and this time he had a worthy witchy opponent. If his plan worked, Stella would find out what it was like to be ugly inside AND out!

Chapter Fourteen

*P*sst!
Trix felt a rush of air at her ear.

Psst!

Has one of Lulu's blue-winged dragonflies escaped again? Trix wondered. The shimmer from their wings was used in all kinds of potions.

Psst!

There was that sound again so very close

to her ear. She gently waved her hand. She didn't want to hurt the dragonfly, but it was distracting her from what Lulu was saying and Trix was already distracted big-time. She'd made her best friend invisible and told her that she, Trix, was a witch. That was breaking multiple Sisterhood of Magic rules. Trix hated breaking the rules and keeping secrets. And she hated how worry and guilt were now gurgling in her tummy like the ingredients in Lulu's cauldron. What was she going to do?

Psst! "Trix." It was Holly's voice.

Oh, no! Trix's situation had gone from bad to super-duper disaster. Her best friend had sneaked into the magic classroom! How could Trix keep invisible Holly a secret from Lulu? Lulu always seemed to know everything. Part of Trix *wanted* to tell Lulu – she would know what to do – but the other part wanted to find a way to make Holly visible again without anyone finding out about Trix's rule-breaking. If she told Lulu, it was sure to mean the end to Trix's hopes of a fairy godmother future. It was as if breaking the rules had been a bad seed that had now sprouted jagged roots and spiky thorns. Trix felt caught in this prickly mess and she wasn't sure how to get out of it.

"Trix," Holly said again, right into Trix's ear, "watch out for Stella."

Trix wanted to ask a million questions but how could she speak without drawing attention to herself?

Holly's hand fumbled for Trix's. Trix took Holly's hand and squeezed it. As long as Holly was her best friend, everything would be all right.

"Everyone happy?" Lulu asked with a twirl and a jingle-jangle of her bracelets.

Trix wasn't exactly happy. She was pleased there were no more secrets between her and Holly, but now she had a whole new batch of secrets to keep.

"Let's see your Happy Potions," Lulu said as she walked around the room inspecting everyone's test tubes.

With trembling fingers, Trix pulled the test tube from her blazer pocket and held up the dark mixture.

"Hmmmm," Lulu said as she studied Trix's potion.

Does she know my Happy Potion makes people invisible? Trix thought, trying not to panic. *Has she guessed that I used it on Holly? Can she sense that invisible Holly is standing right beside her?*

Trix's face flushed.

"Trix, my darling, I think we have a

problem," Lulu said and slipped the tube from Trix's grasp.

Trix pressed her lips together. She wanted to tell Lulu everything. She wanted to tell her so badly it almost hurt to keep the words trapped inside. She squeezed Holly's hand and Holly squeezed back.

"Happy Potions are usually a sunny yellow or a dazzling orange," Lulu said as she swirled the mixture in the tube. "What ingredients did you use?"

"Well, I used some of Jinx's sparkle and a hair from my best friend." Trix tried to smile but her lips felt stiff and twitchy. "And I used snowflakes from your jar of newly fallen snow."

"I'll need to use my magical microscope to see what else has sneaked in here," Lulu said, and Trix thought she glanced in Stella's direction. "Now, where is it?"

Lulu walked over to a battered old wardrobe at the back of the room. "I think it's in here somewhere. I used it last when my Truly Truthful Potion somehow made people tell silly little lies."

Truly Truthful Potion? Those words made Trix's tummy wibble and wobble. Holly must have known how Trix was feeling because she squeezed her hand again.

"Of course, I had mixed a drop of purely pearly honesty with a smidge of little white lie. Easy mistake, of course, they look very similar and, silly me, I forgot to read the labels." She continued to dig in the wardrobe, tossing out strange objects as she searched: a deflated rugby ball, a bouquet of peacock feathers and something that looked like a stethoscope but with a gemstone at the end. "It *must* be here somewhere," she called as she kept searching through the old wardrobe.

Trix was so caught up with watching Lulu and worrying that she didn't see Stella until it was almost too late.

But, thankfully, Jinx and Holly had spotted Stella as she uncorked her test tube of foul-smelling green liquid.

Now Holly shoved Trix out of the way and Jinx dived for Stella's pretty pink shoes. Stella became tangled in a Jinx knot.

Trix stared at the tube in Stella's hand. The
contents swished and sloshed. Stella stumbled
but Cara and Becka kept their friend from
falling. Unfortunately they each caught one
of Stella's arms and the test tube went flying!

Trix thought of the advanced-magic-time-slowing spell, but she was probably in too much trouble already and a cheeky part of her wanted to see what the potion – that Stella had clearly intended for her – would do.

The tube seemed to tumble in slow motion. Stella twisted free and snatched it from the air. But three perfect drops of the potion sloshed out of the tube and kerplopped right on the noses of Stella, Cara and Becka.

Stella stared cross-eyed at the gooey green gunk on the tip of her nose – and screamed.

Chapter Fifteen

Pop! Pop! Pop!
Purple warts burst onto Stella, Cara
and Becka's faces. The girls gaped and
pointed at each other as they turned from
cover girls to Halloween creatures. Their
normally silky hair bushed into stringy
straw which was the most hideous shade
of green Trix had ever seen. The girls'
eyebrows fell out and their skin turned orange.

Stella's ears ballooned to look like an elephant's. Cara's nose grew beak-like, and Becka's eyes bugged out like a frog's.

Trix knew it was mean, but she couldn't help laughing. After all, those slimy drops of Stella's potion had been meant for her. If it hadn't been for Holly and Jinx, she would be the one looking like a cartoon monster. She glanced at Pippa, who was giggling, too!

Lulu turned around, holding what must have been the magical microscope. She gasped. "What is the meaning of this?"

Jinx raced over to Lulu and leaped into her arms. They were nose to nose. Jinx had a magical connection with Lulu. He seemed to be telling her everything. Lulu nodded and glanced at Stella and then over to Trix.

"I see," she said at last. She collected Trix and Stella's potions. Lulu's silence was scary. Lulu studied the potions under the magical microscope, which looked like a normal microscope but emitted a bright sunburst of laser light.

Trix felt the rush of tears. This was it. She would never, ever be a fairy godmother. Her heart felt as if it were wilting, but she sniffed back the sadness. She would not cry in front of those awful wart-faced girls.

"It's going to be fine," Holly whispered to her. "We're in this together now."

That – and the fact that Stella looked as ugly outside as she was inside – made Trix feel a tiny bit better.

"Stella," Lulu said, "I believe you can shed some light on what has happened here."

Stella's now blood-shot eyes brimmed with tears. "I only meant it as a joke."

"Potions are a serious business." Lulu

paced in front of the monstrous versions of Stella, Cara and Becka. "Would you mind telling me what you sneaked into Trix's potion?"

"Dark of the darkest night," Stella whispered. "I'm sorry, Trix."

Lulu nodded. Then she chanted a spell and pointed a finger past Trix.

Trix turned in time to see an outline of her best friend materialise. Holly shimmered until she was fully visible. She shrank behind Trix.

"Trix, I would like you to explain why you broke the most sacred rule of the Sisterhood of Magic," Lulu said.

"I'm sorry. It was a mistake," Trix explained. "You see, I used a drop of my Happy Potion on Holly and she disappeared. So then I had to tell her everything."

"And then I sneaked in with Jinx when I overheard Stella planning to use an Ugly Potion on Trix," Holly piped up, peeking around Trix.

"I'm sorry, Lulu," Trix said. "I really and

truly thought that Holly might be a witch, too."

"You did?" Holly asked.

"No one's more magical than you, Holly," Trix said. "I tried to test you at your birthday party and—"

"Um, Lulu, what about me?" Stella interrupted. Cara and Becka gave her dirty looks. "I mean *us*. What about *us*?" Stella quickly amended. "Don't you have a spell to return us to normal?"

"Stella, I *will* turn you back, but I think it's a fitting punishment that you stay as you are for the moment. Your ugly behaviour has made you ugly." Lulu magicked a mirror in front of Stella, who shrieked and turned away.

Trix felt lighter because she had told Lulu the truth about Holly. She knew that she couldn't stop now. "Lulu, I need to tell you something else," she said, stepping closer to Lulu and stretching up on her tippy-toes. Lulu leaned down so that Trix could whisper in her ear. "I may have used a teeny tiny bit of advanced magic. I didn't mean to. It just popped out. It wasn't exactly an emergency . . ." She broke off, unsure how to continue.

Oh, this is all sounding terrible, Trix thought. She didn't know how to explain it so Lulu would understand that it had all been an accident. And then it might seem to Lulu that Trix was having a lot of magical accidents lately.

Lulu placed a hand on Trix's shoulder. "I appreciate your honesty. Honesty can be the scissors when lies have tied you in knots."

Trix held her breath as Lulu seemed to be thinking what to do next.

"I understand and all is forgiven, but you need to make sure that you don't accidentally use advanced magic until I've instructed you on it properly. And you may not tell anyone else that you are a witch," Lulu told her. "Make new mistakes. Don't re-use old ones."

"Thank you, Lulu," Trix said.

"Well, I have a bit of a dilemma," Lulu said

and started to pace. "Holly, you know a secret you should not. Few non-magical people know about the Sisterhood of Magic." She stopped in front of Holly. "I'm sorry but you do not have the gift of magic, Holly."

Trix felt the sting of disappointment.

"I could mix up my Frightfully Forgetful Potion," Lulu said and scratched at her temple. "But that's a tricky one. It makes holes in your memory. You might also forget what you had for lunch, or what you learned in History last week."

Holly stepped up next to Trix. "I can keep a secret, Lulu. I'm a good secret-keeper." Holly's face flushed but she stood straight and tall. "But, if it's OK, I'd rather not have any secrets from my best friend."

Lulu put one arm around Holly and the other around Trix. "Yes, you are right. Secrets between friends make a different kind of hole, don't they? They poke holes in your trust and in your heart. We can't have that, especially in the truly magical friendship the

two of you have. I will ask the Sisterhood
of Magic for a special exception in the
exceptional case of Miss Holly Duffy. I will
make you an honorary witch!"

Trix and Holly looked at each other as
surprise lit up their faces.

"Holly is a loyal friend with a kind heart
and magical instincts, as she demonstrated
here today – unlike other witches, who don't
seem to understand the difference between

helping and hurting." Lulu glared at Stella, whose feet had now grown to the size and shape of ping-pong paddles. "Trix and Holly can work as a team."

"Oh," Holly squealed. "Will I get magic lessons too?"

Lulu shook her head. "No, I am sorry. The rules are clear on this matter. But you and Trix can work together to help others – Trix with magic and you, Holly, with human kindness."

"But, miss," Stella piped up. "That's not fair. Only witches—"

Lulu raised her hand to stop Stella. "Purple-warted people should consider their own reflection before worrying about what others can or can't do."

Trix stifled a laugh.

Lulu took hold of Holly's hands. "Do you solemnly swear to keep the Sisterhood of Magic a secret and promise never to reveal the existence of witches?"

"I swear," Holly said. "Cross my heart and hope to kiss a purple-warted, green-faced, slime-covered monster." Holly glanced at Stella. "No offence."

Lulu kissed Holly on both cheeks. "You and Trix have a lot to catch up on. Off you go." She turned to Pippa. "I might need a little help. Pippa, would you mind staying and lending me a hand?"

Pippa nodded, unable to take her eyes off Stella, Cara and Becka, who were getting uglier by the minute.

"I have to find a counter-potion for Stella's horrid mixture. And this could get ugly." Lulu paused and smiled a cheeky smile. "Or, should I say, uglier."

Trix, Holly and Jinx turned to leave.

"Are you disappointed that I'm a witch and you're not?" Trix whispered to her friend.

Holly shrugged. "A little, maybe, but you know the next best thing to being a witch?"

"What?" Trix asked.

"Having a best friend who's going to be the most amazing fairy godmother in the world!" Holly said, and then added, "With my help, of course."

The girls laughed as they headed out of the magic classroom and into the library. Trix glanced over her shoulder for one last look at Stella.

"Now . . ." Lulu was facing Stella and the other wart-faced girls. "Let me see . . ." She strolled over to her bookcase. "This may take some time." She picked up a jar full of crusty brown bits. "And you might have to eat a few buffalo toenails covered in the mud from a London puddle."

"Ewww!" the girls screamed and clutched one another.

Trix saw a smile twinkle on Lulu's lips. Lulu was going to have a bit of fun with Stella, Cara and Becka before she returned the girls to normal. Maybe it would teach them to be a little less mean. Trix knew she'd learned her lesson – don't try to keep secrets from Lulu. She felt lucky that Lulu had been able to make Holly visible again, and even luckier that she'd decided to let Holly share Trix's secret. At least something good had come out of her magical mess-up – Holly finally knew Trix was a witch. If Trix could bottle what she was feeling right now, it would be the best Happy Potion ever.

Don't miss the next exciting adventure
in the *Magic Trix* series

Museum Mayhem

Available July 2013!
Read on for a special preview of the first
chapters.

Chapter One

With a flash of light, a puff of blue smoke and a soft *poof*, the tiny grey mouse transformed into a . . .

Trix rubbed her eyes. She must be dreaming. Her brain was whirling like a spinning top. The tiny grey mouse had been replaced by a real, live unicorn. Its spiral horn twinkled in the light of the magic classroom.

Trix had recently turned ten years old and discovered she was a witch. She hoped she never, ever got used to the magic of being magical. Trix stroked the unicorn's silky mane. The animal smelled sugary, like fairy cakes, and it was surrounded by a halo of light.

"Today's lesson will focus on transformations," Lulu said. Every week day, Trix and four other new witches gathered in the secret room in the Little Witching Primary School library. Lulu instructed them on how to use their new powers. The best and brightest witches would become fairy godmothers one day.

"Are transform-whatevers like magical makeovers?" Pippa asked, twisting the curl of her high ponytail around and around her finger.

"Transformations," Lulu corrected, "are not the same as makeovers."

Stella stepped away from the unicorn. "I'm not keen on animals, but I'm a star at makeovers." She pointed at Cara and Becka and whispered, *"Sparkle, glitter, shimmer, shine. No more ugly. It's make-over time."*

A glimmer of light shot from her fingertip and exploded in a shower of pink glitter right over Cara and Becka. When the air cleared, Cara and Becka looked less like ten-year-old girls and more like film stars. Cara's low ponytail had twisted up into a sophisticated bun. Becka's hair was no longer plaited but

fluffed into a massive helmet of curls. Their school uniforms were replaced with long, shimmering gowns.

Trix wasn't sure Stella's makeovers were improvements. Cara and Becka were much prettier without the make-up.

"The transformations I'm talking about are to help you out of tricky situations, not prepare you for fashion magazines," Lulu said and then whispered a spell in the unicorn's ear.

Poof!

The unicorn was once again a tiny grey mouse.

Lulu reached down so the mouse could scamper up her arm. "Thank you, Nester," Lulu said to the mouse, who curled up like an ornament on Lulu's witch's hat. "Transforming living, breathing creatures is very advanced. The practice dates back to Cinderella's fairy godmother, who turned mice into horses and pumpkins into carriages. Today we will start with something simple." She whispered a spell and pointed at the ceiling, moving her finger in a curlicue pattern which set the bangles on her wrist jingle-jangling. Fluffy white clouds appeared overhead. "We will turn rain to snow," Lulu told her witches-in-training.

Maybe it was the magic sparking in the room around her, but Trix's nose twitched and then itched. She rubbed her nose but it still felt tingly, as if she were going to sneeze. Oh, no, she couldn't be getting ill. Her family and her best friend Holly had plans to go to the Natural History Museum in London tomorrow. She couldn't wait to see all the museum's weird and wonderful creatures – especially the dinosaurs!

"With a little help from your familiars," Lulu continued, "dreary rain will become glistening snow."

Familiars raced to their witches. The lavender rat named Twitch scampered over to Pippa. Tabby the cat hopped next to Cara. Sherlock the owl perched on Becka's shoulder, while Rascal, Stella's rambunctious pug, chased his curly tail near Stella's feet. Trix's familiar, a black and white kitten named Jinx, knocked his head against Trix's leg.

"The key to transformations is to imagine your outcome. So start thinking of snow as you say this simple spell." Lulu flicked her wrist and clicked her fingers and it began to rain. Fat drops poured down all around them, bouncing on the shelves of Lulu's magical ingredients and collecting in the cauldron. *I call upon magic – and I must insist. Change the item before me from that to this.*

The girls quickly repeated Lulu's magical spell while dodging raindrops. Jinx wiggled his whiskers, which was his way of boosting Trix's magic. The raindrops changed in mid-air to glistening white snowflakes.

Trix's nose itched and twitched. Trix covered her mouth. Creeping cats, she was going to sn . . . sn . . . sneeze.

Atchoo!

Stella scooted away from Trix. "You are so disgusting," she muttered to Trix. "Keep your germs away from me."

Pippa reached into her pink handbag and handed Trix a tissue just as her nose tingled with another sneeze.

"Th . . . th . . . thanks," Trix blurted and sneezed again.

But now the delicate crystal snowflakes had become sticky green blobs. *Splat! Splat! Splat!* The girls and their familiars were getting covered with green dots.

"Magic marbles," Lulu said, and quickly conjured a lacy parasol to shield herself. "Something's gone magically amiss."

"How perfectly revolting!" Stella exclaimed, diving behind Cara and Becka. She flipped up the trailing skirts of their lovely gowns so that she was sheltered from the goo, but her friends were slowly turning a slimy green from the ooey-gooey rain.

Trix was overwhelmed by the smell of lime. She tilted her head back and stuck out her tongue to catch one green blob and then two. "Yum!" she said, licking the green blotches off her lips. "Lime jelly, my favourite!"

Trix had a sneaking suspicion that she had somehow caused the lime-green mess, but she didn't know how. She hadn't even been thinking of jelly. She had definitely been thinking of snow. Then again, she did have a gift for creating magical messes.

"Let's try to change this back to snow," Lulu said and the girls repeated the transformation spell again.

In a flash, the green in the air and on their clothes, hair and skin became soft white snow once more.

"I'm not sure what happened there,"

Lulu said, closing her parasol. "But my demonstration has revealed a gap in your witchy education and it must be addressed immediately."

"I agree, miss," Stella said and smoothed her perfectly straightened hair. "It's obvious that some witches can't even perform the simplest spells." She glared right at Trix. "I think Trix definitely needs some lessons on style and—"

Trix wished she could transform Stella into a nicer person – or maybe a farm animal.

"It is obvious," Lulu interrupted Stella's list of Trix's areas for improvement, "that some of you need to brush up on your people skills." Lulu directed the pointy end of her brolly right at Stella. "If you hope to be fairy godmothers one day, you will need kind hearts and giving natures. Your assignment for this weekend is to perform as many random acts of kindness as you can." Stella groaned and Lulu glared at her. "And you are not allowed to use magic in your kind acts."

Stella groaned again. "I'd rather learn transformations," she muttered.

Trix felt as giddy as she did on Christmas Day when it was time to open presents. Tomorrow she'd have the perfect place to be randomly kind. She was travelling to London and visiting the Natural History Museum – surely there would be millions of people to help in the big city.

But Trix never could have guessed that her random acts would turn out to be more dangerous than a T-Rex.

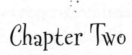

Chapter Two

If Trix's excitement were ice cream, it would
fill the Atlantic Ocean. She was on a train
to London! "I want to see the dinosaurs
and the Wildlife Garden and the big blue
whale and the . . ." she continued to list
nearly everything she'd seen on the museum
website.

"I don't want to see any creepy-crawlies,"
Holly said as they bounced in their seats like

rubber ducks on a sea of fizzy lemonade.
"Can we please visit the gift shop? I love a
gift shop!"

Trix's little brother Oscar popped up from
the seat behind them. He must have been
hiding there since they'd left Little Witching.
"You two belong in a museum," he said.
"You'd be in the stupid and ugly exhibition!"
Oscar clutched his sides, laughing.

"Oh, go away and leave us alone," Trix
muttered so their parents couldn't hear her.

Oscar hopped up on his seat and grabbed
for the luggage
rack above.
"Look!
I bet I
could do
six million
pull-ups.
Or maybe
I could fit
up there!"
Oscar hauled
himself up.

Mum and Dad were sitting a few rows ahead. Mum was reading the glossy magazine that she always kept in her massive handbag. "Oscar, stop it this instant!" she said without even glancing up.

Oscar dropped back down to the floor and swiped Trix's green, draw-string rucksack. He swung it over his head before Dad snatched it and returned it to Trix.

"Oscar, why don't you come and sit with me?" Dad said and scooted over to make room for Oscar next to him.

"Spending all day with Oscar the Horrible is worse than diving into a swimming pool of slime," Trix whispered to Holly.

"Filled with frogs," Holly added with a giggle.

"And sprinkled with toenails," Trix finished and the girls squealed in disgust.

Meow!

That had to be Jinx. Only witches could see and hear him. Lulu had cast a spell to make him invisible. Trix wasn't allowed an ordinary cat because Dad was allergic. Jinx loved a game of hide and seek – and so did Trix – but Jinx was always the one hiding and Trix the one seeking. Where could he be? She looked under the seats and then stood on tiptoes to peer in the luggage rack.

"Are you looking for Jinx?" Holly whispered. She'd only recently found out that Trix was a witch with an invisible familiar.

Trix nodded.

"Lost your brain again, weirdo?" Oscar shouted at Trix. "It's so small you'll never find it!" He laughed hysterically.

"At least I *have* a brain," Trix called back.

"I thought your witchy homework was to perform random acts of *kindness*," Holly reminded Trix.

"Not for my brother," Trix replied through gritted teeth. "He's lucky I don't perform *planned* acts of *evil*."

Meow!

Trix spotted Jinx at last. He was batting a broken red button up and down the aisle, ducking and diving around passengers' shoes.

She smiled at Jinx and all her frustration with Oscar faded away.

The train jolted to a stop at the next station. People poured into all the empty seats and spaces, like custard covering apple crumble. Trix noticed a grey-haired lady shuffling onto the crowded train as the doors thudded shut. "Oh, dearie me," she mumbled. A bead of sweat trickled down her brow from her mop of silvery curls.

Now was Trix's chance for kindness.

"Excuse me!" Trix yelled as she pushed through the maze of passengers. She was jostled by the train's motion and bumped by cases and handbags. She felt as if she were running up hill through an avalanche of smelly fish but she nudged and elbowed her way through until she was face to face with the old lady.

"Hello," Trix said and smiled the sweetest smile she could muster in the hot and stinky train. "Why don't you take my seat?"

The old lady's face changed. The wrinkles that seemed to weigh her down lifted with a smile. "Thank you, dear," she said and patted Trix's cheek. Her touch was feather light and she smelled of the expensive perfume Trix and Holly had tested last time they went shopping with Mum.

"Follow me!" Trix said and cleared a path.

The old lady sat down in the seat next to Holly. "Thank you again," the lady said. "That was very kind of you."

Zing! The most thrilling feeling rushed through Trix. She loved the way everyone was looking at her and smiling. She'd done a good deed for one person but that good feeling appeared to have spread throughout the whole train carriage.

Trix squeezed in next to Holly and pressed herself against the window as the train rumbled towards London. She watched as the leafy trees and golden fields gave way to buildings that crunched closer together and reached higher and higher with every passing mile.

The last time she'd visited London, she'd been making a secret midnight flight on her witch's broomstick. She remembered how beautiful London had looked at night with all its twinkling lights. She wondered if London would be as magical from the ground in the daylight.

As the conductor announced that the next stop was the train's final destination, Trix's nose began to itch and twitch. She could feel a sneeze gathering momentum.

The train slowed and the buildings of London came into focus. One was shaped like a gherkin, another resembled a spike of broken glass and a third looked like the billowing sail of a pirate ship.

Trix pinched her nose with one hand and covered her mouth with the other but the sneezy feeling kept growing and growing until . . .

A . . . a . . . atchoo!

"Was that you, Trix?" Mum called. "I hope you aren't getting ill."

"I'm fine," Trix replied but her attention was drawn to the strangest sight. She blinked and blinked again. One of the buildings up

ahead had an elephant's trunk, a rabbit's ears and a cat's whiskers. How did they make buildings like *that*?

Another sneeze rushed over her like a rocket. The feeling and the sneeze came in one big whoosh!

Atchoo!

She couldn't be getting ill – not today.

The train came to a stop. Trix looked back for the mixed-up animal building but she couldn't spot it anywhere. Maybe she'd imagined it – or maybe London truly was a magical place.